Dear readers and friends,

It's time to wrap up this book, and I'm truly thankful for having shared this journey with you. Your support and companionship have been the driving force behind completing this effort, and I deeply appreciate your gratitude and commitment.

This book isn't just a conversation between us; it's a success story we've all contributed to. While writing, I felt the encouragement and inspiration from all of you, which played a significant role in achieving new heights.

With this dedication, I want to express my sincere thanks to all readers, family members, and everyone who was part of this successful journey. Being on this journey with you has created a special connection between me, you, and the book.

Thanks to everyone who included my book in their reading list, making it part of our shared conversation. I hope this book brings positive changes to your life, and you find joy in its contents.

Thanks to each one of you, and best wishes to all.

Sincerely,

Sunil Govind Kotwal

THE SECRET OF BLISSFULL HEALTH : YOUR PATH TO HAPPINESS

SUNIL GOVIND KOTWAL

Copyright © SUNIL GOVIND KOTWAL
All Rights Reserved.

This book has been self-published with all reasonable efforts taken to make the material error-free by the author. No part of this book shall be used, reproduced in any manner whatsoever without written permission from the author, except in the case of brief quotations embodied in critical articles and reviews.

The Author of this book is solely responsible and liable for its content including but not limited to the views, representations, descriptions, statements, information, opinions and references ["Content"]. The Content of this book shall not constitute or be construed or deemed to reflect the opinion or expression of the Publisher or Editor. Neither the Publisher nor Editor endorse or approve the Content of this book or guarantee the reliability, accuracy or completeness of the Content published herein and do not make any representations or warranties of any kind, express or implied, including but not limited to the implied warranties of merchantability, fitness for a particular purpose. The Publisher and Editor shall not be liable whatsoever for any errors, omissions, whether such errors or omissions result from negligence, accident, or any other cause or claims for loss or damages of any kind, including without limitation, indirect or consequential loss or damage arising out of use, inability to use, or about the reliability, accuracy or sufficiency of the information contained in this book.

Made with ♥ on the Notion Press Platform
www.notionpress.com

Contents

Preface

In the tapestry of life, where health and spirituality interlace, this book emerges as a guide to unravel the threads that weave these integral aspects of our existence. As we navigate the fast-paced currents of contemporary living, the significance of maintaining a harmonious balance between our physical well-being and spiritual fulfillment becomes ever more pronounced.

Journey to Wholeness is an exploration, a humble attempt to redefine our understanding of health and happiness. It delves into the intricate relationship between the body, mind, and soul, uncovering the profound impact they have on our overall well-being. In a world inundated with complexities, this book seeks to offer a beacon of simplicity—an invitation to rediscover the innate wisdom within ourselves.

The chapters within are not just words on paper; they are stepping stones towards a life of vitality and contentment. We delve into the essence of meditation, the power of positive thinking, and the transformative influence of embracing natural healing practices like Ayurveda. It is an odyssey toward a medication-free existence, a return to the fundamental connection between our well-being and the world around us.

Nirvana, often seen as an elusive goal, is presented here not as a destination but as an ever-present spiritual truth. It unifies the principles of nature, care, nourishment, and natural healing, guiding us on a serene journey towards prosperity. As we immerse ourselves in this exploration, the book endeavors to connect the dots of our lives—a mosaic where nature, nourishment, care, and spirituality create a harmonious symphony.

This is an invitation to pause, reflect, and embark on a journey towards a wholesome life. It is a celebration of the interconnectedness of body, mind, and soul—a journey that aligns us with the universal rhythms.

May this book serve as a companion on your path to a fulfilling and healthy life.

Warm regards,
Sunil Govind Kotwal

Acknowledgements

I extend my heartfelt gratitude to everyone who contributed to the realization of this book. Writing and completing this work has been a collaborative effort, and I would like to express my appreciation to those who supported and inspired me throughout this journey.

First and foremost, I express my gratitude to Sirshreeji, my spiritual guru and the founder of Tejgyan Foundation: Happy Thoughts, for his divine blessings and inner guidance, which empowered me to write this book.

I want to thank my readers – your interest in this book has been the driving force behind its creation. Your engagement and feedback have been invaluable, motivating me to present the best possible content.

I am deeply thankful to my parrents, my wife Kavita, my family and friends for their unwavering support. Your encouragement, understanding, and patience during the writing process have been crucial. Special thanks to Kedar P sir, Rupa Bunnar mam and Pritam Patil sir and his community for their valuable insights and constructive feedback.

I express my gratitude to Prime Time community for their guidance and support in shaping this work. Their expertise and encouragement have been instrumental in refining the content.

Last but not least, I want to thank the entire publishing team of Notion Press and everyone involved in the production of this book. Your dedication and hard work have played a pivotal role in bringing this project to fruition.

This book stands as a collective achievement, and I am sincerely thankful to each one of you who played a part, directly or indirectly, in making it a reality.

With gratitude,
Sunil Govind Kotwal

About The Author

I am Sunil Kotwal, a government official, certified Naturopathy practitioner, health studies enthusiast, and author with over 25 years of extensive experience in the finance department of government service. I have served in various departments in Maharashtra. Eleven years ago, I experienced a heart attack, which was surprising as I had no such habits. To understand this, I participated in a Naturopathy camp at India's most popular Naturopathy ashram, where I appreciated the lifestyle and various treatments.

I have a fondness for Naturopathy and obtained a diploma from a renowned Naturopathy institution. Subsequently, I started learning and practicing about human health, herbalogy, acupuncture, sound healing meditation, spirituality, and their interconnections. My goal is to provide advice and guidance based on my real experiences so that solutions can be found for upcoming challenges. I want what I have learned to be useful for all those facing health issues.

During my journey, the challenges I faced became the reason for my desire to save others from similar struggles. I did not want others to go through the same thoughts and actions that I did. The knowledge accumulated during my tenure is now something I am proud of, and I am eager to share it with those who are still facing similar struggles.

Sunil Govind Kotwal
BCom, LLB, DPM, ND
Mob: 8888082960
Email: sgk192@gmail.com

The Power Of 5n Nature, Nurture, Nutrients, Naturopathy & Nirvana

1. **Nature**:This word is associated with nature and natural elements, specifically indicating natural phenomena and processes that occur in the natural environment.

2. **Nurture**:The meaning of the word "Nurture" is to support and care. It denotes the action of keeping a person or thing safe, fostering development, and providing encouragement.

3. **Nutrients**:Nutrients are those essential elements in food that assist the body in providing energy, nourishment, and support. Examples include vitamins, minerals, and proteins.

4. **Naturopathy**:Naturopathy is a holistic medical approach that advocates treating diseases with natural remedies, diet, and other natural elements.

5. **Nirvana**:Nirvana is a religious and philosophical term that signifies an elevated state or liberation, where an individual becomes free from ignorance and suffering, reaching a state of perfection or tranquility.

Nature, Nurturing, Naturopathy, Nutrients, and Nirvana - these five words together convey meaningful insights into the direction of perfection and a healthy life."

Introduction: Health And Spirituality

In today's lifestyle, the importance of health and spirituality is increasing. It perceives health not only in terms of physical well-being but also guides us towards a balanced and joyful life with mental and spiritual health. To achieve a successful and fulfilling life, we can focus on various aspects.

1. **The Secret of Prosperity: Health and Happiness**

Explore the wonderful connection between solutions and well-being for a happy and healthy life.

2. **Prevention and Solution of Physical Illness**

Study the ways to stay physically healthy through proper nutrition, regular exercise, and ideal physical care.

3. **Secrets of Nutrients: The Significance of Diet for Health**

Understand the essential secrets for a healthy life by incorporating the right nutrients into your diet.

4. **Body, Mind, and Soul: Balance**

Recognize the importance of relationships between the body, mind, and soul for a balanced and happy life.

5. **Meditation: Like a Medicine**

Understand the importance of meditation for attaining peace and health with Ayurvedic principles.

6. **Acupuncture and Sound Healing: Using Sound for Health**

Learn how to use sound for better physical and mental health with acupuncture and sound healing.

7. **Consistency: The Key to Stability and Success**

Understand the importance of consistency in life and how it can lead to stability and success.

8. **Medication-Free Living**

Move forward towards a positive and balanced life with a medication-free lifestyle.

9. **Health and Spirituality: The Intersection of Health and Spirituality**

These two crucial aspects profoundly impact experienced and focused human life.

10. **Nirvana: A Philosophical and Spiritual Concept**

According to the principles of Nirvana, it is a state of spiritual liberation and the perfection of the soul.

Through these unique topics, we can make life joyful and positive.

ONE

Chapter 1: The Path to a Happy and Healthy Life

Nature

1) Five Pillars of Health: Ensuring Overall Well-being

The foundation of our body is based on five main pillars, namely food, sleep, water, physical activity, and positive thinking. If these pillars are strong, we can lead a healthy life throughout.

The first pillar is Food or Nutrition.

Food is what we consume to keep our physical health intact and to gain energy. It is made up of various food substances such as lentils, rice, vegetables, fruits, milk, grains, meat, and many more. Consuming a healthy diet provides us with energy and helps maintain our physical and mental health. Determining what to eat, when to eat, and how much to eat is crucial.

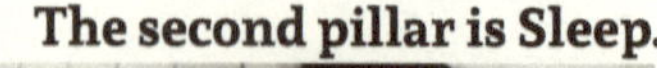

The second pillar is Sleep.

The quality of sleep is essential, not just the quantity. It is important to sleep at the right time, ideally from 10 PM to 5 AM. Our physical and mental biological clock is set according to this time. Proper sleep benefits us, providing freshness in the morning and enabling us to perform well throughout the day. Sleeping or resting at night is a vital physical necessity that rejuvenates us, providing us with energy and preparing us for the next day.

The third pillar is Water.

It is crucial to consume the right amount of water throughout the day. For every 20 kilograms of weight, one liter of water is recommended. For instance, if your weight is 60 kilograms, three liters of water daily is sufficient. Drinking water in the morning is better than sipping it while sitting or before or after meals. Hydrated water helps keep our body cool and supports proper bodily functions.

The fourth pillar is Exercise, Physical Activity.

Engaging in the right amount of physical activity is crucial for us. It provides proper exercise to every part of our body, making it healthy and strong. Regular exercise provides us with energy, enhances mental health, and aids in weight management. Regular exercise helps prevent diseases and can make life positive and vibrant. Physical activities contribute to maintaining our physical health, including various forms of exercise such as running, exercise, yoga, and sports. Exercising can increase physical activity, strengthen muscles, and help maintain physical health.

The fifth pillar is Positive Thinking.

Our thoughts should be positive. Positive thinking enables us to find solutions to problems in the right way. Its impact is also on our physical health. "Positive thinking" refers to a mental state in which a person views things with a positive and enthusiastic perspective and sees competition, problems, and challenges in a positive way. Positive thinking motivates a person to improve, learn, and grow. It enhances enthusiasm, self-confidence, and a sense of support.

In summary, focusing on these five pillars - Nutrition, Sleep, Water, Exercise, and Positive Thinking - can pave the way for a happy and healthy life.

2) Importance of the Five Pillars of Health: A Direction towards Prosperous and Sustainable Living

We have understood how crucial food, sleep, adequate water intake, positive thinking, and physical activity are in our lives. Using all these in the right proportion helps maintain the balance of our body and improves our physical health. We can live a healthy life throughout, and if we do not have any illness, we do not need any medication. This helps us avoid the side effects of medicines. Living a healthy life brings us mental peace, mental resolution, and also enhances our family's health.

3) Fundamental Components of Health: Keys to a Positive and Prosperous Life

By maintaining these five elements in the right way, we can progress towards a happy and prosperous life. It is true that proper nutrition and appropriate exercise are essential for our body. To live a healthy life, we should eat at the right time and know how to provide our body with the right amount of water, food, and exercise.

Additionally, sleep is also important, and it should be at the right time. Sleeping and waking up according to the biological clock can be very beneficial for maintaining our physical health, allowing us to lead a good life.

If we follow the **"80-20 rule,"** (focus 80%on right food and 20 % on physical activity) our physical and mental health will be better. Meditation is also a good way to improve our mental health. Keep in mind that all these things can help us in the direction of a healthy and happy life. It is crucial to keep your thoughts and actions positive to maintain everything.

4) Health is Wealth: A Positive Perspective

Health is Wealth; our physical health is our greatest asset, so it is said that it should be given top priority. If our physical health is good, we can save on the expenses of medicine, pharmacies, and hospitals. Good health provides us with the ability to think and work positively.

Taking care of our physical health can enhance our productivity and boost our confidence. If our health is good, we can perform better in our work, increasing the chances of salary increments and promotions. Maintaining physical health can help us avoid illnesses, saving on hospital admission costs. It can also reduce expenses related to the side effects of medications.

Protecting our physical health makes our family feel secure, and the money saved from medical expenses can be used for other family needs. In this way, taking care of health can help us in our financial situation.

5) Fundamental Components of Health: Keys to a Positive and Prosperous Life

Health is crucial for our life. Sirshreeji (founder of Tejgyan foundation popularly known as Happy thoughts) says, "If health is a question, then the answer is the **answer.**" The acronym ANSWER stands for **A**ir, **N**utrients, **S**ilence, **W**ater, **E**xercise, and **R**elaxation. Maintaining a proper balance of all these elements is necessary.

Sleep is a natural and the biggest form of relaxation, which comes in abundance with air, water, and nutrients. Using it correctly is beneficial for us. Additionally, incorporating silence or meditation into our lives is also important. Physical activity and exercise are essential for our body to function properly. Along with this, quality sleep, not just quantity, is necessary for good health.

If we follow all these steps correctly, we can lead a healthy and better life without the need for medication. This will keep our energy source intact, allowing us to spend our days positively.

6) Improving Health: A Positive Simple Guide

It is important to cultivate good habits. It is said that a person first creates their habits, and later those habits shape the person. That is, the good habits we develop from childhood contribute to enjoying a healthy life throughout our lives. However, if our habits are not good, we may be prone to illnesses. Therefore, it is essential to adopt good habits from childhood.

For example:

1. Wake up early in the morning
2. Express gratitude for everything
3. Meditate
4. Maintain a positive mindset

5. Engage in physical exercise
6. Reading
7. Read good books
8. Contemplate
9. Eat a balanced diet
10. Stay hydrated
11. Get sufficient sleep
12. Maintain a regular sleep schedule
13. Goal writing
14. Engage in positive self-talk

These habits need to be adopted because good habits lead to efficient time management, savings in every aspect of life, financial stability, and the development of trustworthiness among people. Therefore, it is necessary to maintain consistency in every aspect of our lives.

7) Happy and Healthy Life: A Comprehensive Guide

We have the power within us to make ourselves healthy. Our body and mind are nothing less than a miracle. Our thoughts are powerful, and what we focus on reflects in our lives. We need to focus on what we want, not on what we don't want. If we want to stay away from illness, we should affirm, "I am completely healthy, I am enjoying good health." Instead of saying, "I don't want to be sick," as this directs our attention to the negative aspect and attracts illness towards us.

If any part of our body is in discomfort, we should apologize to that part, seek forgiveness, and express gratitude for the support it has provided us so far. In this way, we can continue to receive support, and we can move ourselves.

8) Healthy and Happy Life: Simple Guidelines

Health is our inherent right, but we have attracted diseases into our lives. We are responsible for it. This indicates that diseases are primarily a result of mental processes, affecting our body adversely. To stay healthy, we need to pay attention to our thoughts.

There is a proverb in Indian literature, 'Healthy mind, and healthy body.' If our mental health is good, we become ideal in society, forming joyful relationships, and becoming role models. We build good relationships with our people, and we manifest in the right direction in society. Additionally, from a spiritual perspective, we become capable. A healthy body helps us in spiritual development.

In this way, our health is not only essential for physical well-being but also for mental, social, and spiritual development.

9) The Secret to a Happy and Healthy Life: Taking Steps in the Right Direction

If we want to live a joyful and healthy life, it is essential to cultivate certain qualities within us. This enables us to enhance our physical capabilities and stay fit. We can contribute significantly to maintaining the health of our body, mind, and society. For this, developing our physical abilities, skills, and efficiency can be effortless, allowing us to experience mental peace. In this way, our mind is inspired towards a joyful and healthy life.

To keep it intact, we need to incorporate activities like meditation and exercise into our lives. This can make us valuable in our family and society, fostering positive relationships with people we come in contact with."

TWO

Chapter 2: Healthy Living Principles: The Secret of Health,Patience, and Nutrients

1) Health Awareness: A Step Towards Good Health

Due to physical health issues, everyone should have basic knowledge about their body so that we can take care of our health. Our body consists of various systems, and each system has its own function. Understanding this helps us comprehend how a problem in any system can impact our health.

Health awareness is crucial because the lack of it is causing us to face various diseases nowadays. Another important factor is the absence of good habits. People often do not know which habits are good for them and which are not. The absence of good habits makes people vulnerable to diseases.

Therefore, it is essential to understand how to interact with our body in a useful and correct way to live a healthy life and adopt good habits.Good habits are an essential part of making life positive. We should understand which habits can be beneficial for us and incorporate them into our lifestyle. We should also keep in mind that in today's fast-paced lifestyle, people often do not pay attention to their physical capabilities. Due to technological advancements, we rely on machines for our physical activities, which may lead to a decrease in our physical activities. To face the challenges ahead, we may need to make changes in our lifestyle."

2) Health Awareness: Making Life Active, Positive, and Secure

Health is the most crucial aspect, and it is essential for us to stay aware of it. Due to this, we need to focus on our fitness and physical capabilities. If our physical fitness is adequate, we can perform all tasks correctly, and our efficiency may increase.Physical capability is the key to identifying health. We need to understand that if our body is healthy, we can use it correctly to fulfill our tasks. This can open up our possibilities entirely, enhancing our productivity, whether we are at home, in the office, or within society.

Therefore, health awareness is necessary for us to ensure our fitness and make our bodies capable.

3) Health Consciousness: Ways to Bring Change Towards a Healthy Life

In today's era, it is necessary for us and our families to be aware of health to live life correctly. For this, we need to ensure that wherever we can find information related to health, we make use of it.Magazines, newspapers, Google, YouTube – we need to use all these technological tools to develop awareness. We should also attend seminars and webinars, which can help increase awareness about health. In today's time, these seminars are often free of cost, and by attending them, we can benefit from the guidance of specialists on various topics and diseases.

4) Worry and Stress: Understanding Their Impact and Coping Mechanisms

Chinta (worry) and Tanav (stress) are like cheetahs that aggressively approach us. Let's study their effects. Stress is an essential part of our lives and is necessary in the right amount. Stress often motivates us to move forward, such as feeling stressed during exam times, leading us to study.

However, excessive stress, strain, and worry can directly impact our physical and mental health.

Avoiding excessive stress is crucial because it can make us sick and can adversely affect our lives. Therefore, it is necessary to eliminate worry and maintain a positive perspective. Sometimes, we get distressed due to negative events in our lives, but we must remember that things will change, and time will heal. To live a stress-free life, we need to stay proactive and remember that **'this too shall pass.'**

5) Worry-Free Living: Towards Peace and Prosperity

Worry plays a significant role in our lives, enabling us to progress and move forward. Controlling worry properly provides us with mental peace, brings solutions, and reduces stress in our actions. Living a life without worry provides us with the benefits of mental and physical health.

Living without worry gives us mental peace, allowing us to channel our energy at the right time and place. This energy helps us maintain the right relationships and guides us towards high levels of performance. In the absence of worry, our mental equilibrium is maintained, leading to improvements in both physical and mental health. Living without worry encourages us to utilize our energy in the right direction and solve problems rather than dwelling on them, thus allowing us to fill our lives with positivity.

6) Worry-Free Living: Towards a Happy and Prosperous Life through Self-Empowerment

To begin with, to live a life without worry, we need to ask ourselves a question - why did this event or person (negative) come into my life, and what is its purpose? Once we find the answer, we can work towards our inner and outer development. So, what is the need to worry?

What will happen by worrying? Instead of worrying, we should use mindfulness or meditation regularly. Taking at least ten minutes every morning for meditation can be beneficial. While reading books, we can read biographies of good leaders, jokes, and comics. Additionally, watching light-hearted comedy movies or TV series can help reduce stress and worry.

NURTURE

Nurture means to provide nourishment or to give life. It signifies the action of keeping someone or something safe, fostering growth, and providing encouragement. An example of nurturing could be assisting someone in their education, development, or progress. It implies caring for the natural development of someone or enhancing their energy and capabilities.

7) The Secret of Nutrients: Information for a Healthy and Positive Life

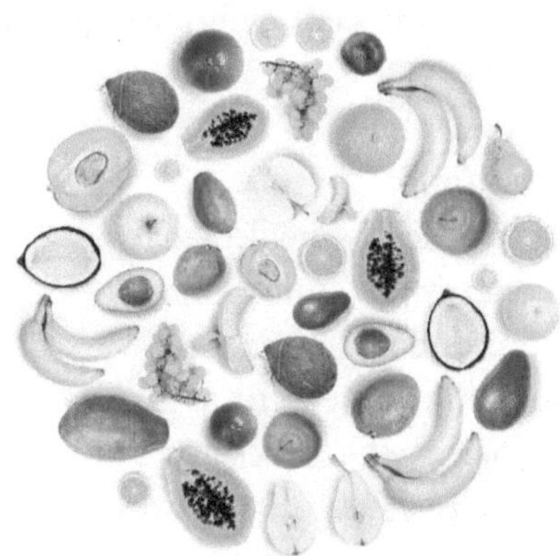

Nutrients play a crucial role in our physical and mental well-being. These elements are essential for maintaining the right bodily functions, sustaining energy levels, and facilitating the development of various organs. For a healthy and positive life, it is necessary to acquire these nutrients in the correct proportion and from the right sources.

Types of Nutrients:

1. Protein:

- Protein is crucial for the excellent structure of the body and for increasing energy.It can be obtained from sources like milk, lentils, and meat.

2. Vitamins and Minerals:

- Vitamins and minerals are necessary for various functions in the body, such as the healthy development of bones and the formation of blood.They can be obtained from vegetables, fruits, eggs, and high-quality food items.

3. Carbohydrates:

- Carbohydrates provide energy to the body and maintain it in the right condition.Cereals, fruits, and vegetables are rich sources of carbohydrates.

4. Fiber:

- Fiber improves physical digestion and keeps the digestive system healthy.It is abundant in lentils, grains, fresh fruits, and vegetables.

5. Fats:

- The right kinds of fats are essential for the body and maintain the correct energy levels. Good-quality oils, especially olive oil, and dry fruits are rich sources of fats.

In conclusion, nurturing involves providing sustenance and support for the natural growth and development of an individual or thing, and understanding the importance of various nutrients contributes to a healthy and positive life.

Practical Suggestions:

- Embrace various nutrient-rich meal options.
- Include maximum natural foods in your diet for healthy eating.
- Regularly review your diet based on energy consumption.
- Consume an adequate amount of water and stay hydrated.

From this study, we can learn that nutrients are essential for the proper functioning of the human body. It emphasizes the necessity of obtaining nutrients in the right proportion to avoid physical discomfort, which is referred to as illness. The types of nutrients include carbohydrates, fiber, fats, protein, vitamins, minerals, and water. A balanced diet ensures the fulfillment of these nutrients, allowing the body's systems to function properly and promoting overall health. If some of these elements are lacking, we may face health issues. Therefore, it is crucial to gather information about all these nutrients and make efforts to achieve their completeness in our diet.

NUTRIENTS

8) Importance of Nutrients: Relevance for a Healthy and Positive Life

For the proper functioning of our body systems, we need the intake of nutritional substances to keep them organized and active. When supplied adequately, we can enjoy good health, and our well-being remains consistently positive. Therefore, it is crucial to consume nutrients in the right proportion.After receiving the right amount of nourishment in the body, it contributes to thoughtful consideration and support in the subsequent functional processes. This leads to the benefits of health, and there is no need for regular medication. We can live a medicine-free life throughout our lifetime.

In cases where our body lacks essential nutrients or faces deficiencies, we encounter various health issues such as anemia, night blindness, etc.

9) Awareness of Nutrients: Measures to Increase Awareness for a Healthy Life

1. Promotion of Healthy Eating Awareness:

Raise awareness among people about the importance of a balanced diet.Highlight the significance of a diet rich in vegetables, fruits, grains, milk, pulses, and protein.

2. Encouragement for Healthy Shopping:

Support local markets and farmers' markets. Promote the consumption of local products that are rich in health and freshness.

3. Education about the Importance of Nutrients:

Educate people about the significance of nutrients through various means.Especially emphasize the importance of nutrients for developing healthy habits among children.

4. Enhancement of Healthy Options in the Kitchen:

- Encourage recipes and options for healthy eating.
- Support techniques for easily preparing healthy food options at home.

5. Promotion of a Healthy Lifestyle:

- Increase awareness about yoga and exercise.
- Explain the growing importance of consuming cold water and encourage people to focus on daily exercise routines.

6. Awareness Programs in Educational Centers:

- Conduct awareness programs on the importance of health in educational centers. Organize annual lectures on the significance of nutrients in schools and colleges.

7. Shareable Content on Social Media:

- Share content on social media platforms promoting the importance of a healthy diet and nutrients.
- Support hashtag campaigns to increase online awareness.

Through these measures, we can enhance awareness of nutrients in society, inspiring everyone towards a healthy lifestyle. Consuming an appropriate diet with adequate nutrients is essential for boosting nutrient levels in our bodies. For this, we should consume a variety of raw vegetables and fruits to get the right amount of fiber and stay hydrated. Additionally, including high-fiber fruits and whole grains in our diet is crucial. We should consume the right amount of Omega-3 fatty acids, found in seasonal fruits and cereals. It is also important to include good sources of protein, such as nuts, chickpeas, and lentils.

Consuming nutrients from the right sources, such as fruits, vegetables, and other natural foods, is also essential. Adequate intake of vitamin B12 is necessary to combat fatigue and weakness caused by its deficiency.

THREE

Chapter 3: Harmony of Body, Mind, and Soul, Meditation, Positive Mindset

1) Direction towards Wholeness: Achieving Capable and Blissful Life through Triteek Balance of Body, Mind, and Soul

Embarking on the path of holistic living: The convergence of Body, Mind, and Soul

To maintain our body in an optimally functioning state, the convergence of Body, Mind, and Soul is crucial. These three are interconnected by an invisible thread, and they contribute to the overall health of the human body. If the body is healthy, mental well-being is sustained, leading to contentment in the soul. From a spiritual perspective, our presence on Earth is for self-development, and we can liberate ourselves from afflictions.

Therefore, it is imperative to keep our body and mind healthy. For this, we need to maintain harmony in three aspects: emotion, thought, and action. We must strive for unity in expression, ensuring that our words align with our thoughts and actions. To achieve this oneness is to become indivisible, free from disparities in speech and action. From a spiritual standpoint, our objective is to work towards our inner development, and we can attain freedom from worldly afflictions.

To accomplish this, it is necessary to maintain unity in our emotions, thoughts, and actions. Becoming indivisible in expression helps to sustain the health of both our body and mind, providing tranquility to our soul. This unity serves as a supportive companion in our spiritual journey.

2) Harmony of Body, Mind, and Soul: The Marvelous Ocean of Joy and Prosperous Life

A suggestion for a fulfilling life is to maintain a harmonious connection between our body, mind, and soul. An individual whose body, mind, and soul are in sync exudes a sense of resolution and balance, akin to a sage or saint. Such a person can effortlessly find solutions to challenges through their experiences.

The structure of the body is similar to that of a person whose body, mind, and soul are in harmony. While all the physical organs and components exist in the body, the presence of mind and soul is not physical; yet, they hold immense power. Our mind has the ability to make anything possible, making humans capable of miracles and leading a joyous life.The soul, being beyond the body and mind, still holds sway over them. By utilizing the soul correctly, we can achieve victory over our life's goals.

3) Living Together in Joyful Harmony: The Connection of Soul, Body, and Mind

Body, mind, and soul constitute significant aspects of our lives. Maintaining their balance aids in keeping our lives joyful. Paying attention to the body, keeping the mind calm, and connecting with the soul contribute to the wholesome integrity of our singular life. Understanding the relationship between body, mind, and soul enables us to steer our lives towards true happiness and prosperity.

Body Connection:

The body is our primary connection that enables us to experience the physical world. Its structure, health, and tangible form significantly impact our lives. Through physical awareness, we can incorporate regular exercise, maintain a healthy diet, and manage our time effectively.

Mind Connection:

The mind governs our emotions, thoughts, and concerns, playing a crucial role in our personal and social experiences. With proper mental health, we can progress towards our goals, achieve a state of balance, and exhibit self-devotion. Practices like yoga, meditation, and positive thinking can enhance mental equilibrium.

Soul Connection:

The soul is our inner self, mysterious, immortal, and infinite. Through the soul, we gain self-awareness and spiritual experiences, allowing us to experience genuine knowledge, love, and peace.

Key to a Healthy Life:

While we have taken various steps for the well-being of our body and mind, it's equally vital to maintain a robust relationship with the soul. To enhance awareness in this regard, we should focus on the following program:

1. Collaborate with our body fully.
2. Regularly benefit from meditation.
3. Ensure quality sleep.
4. Educate ourselves on positive thoughts.
5. Help ourselves and others.
6. Practice self-control.
7. Consume good food and maintain a healthy diet.
8. Cultivate relationships with positive individuals.
9. Read religious and spiritual texts.
10. Enjoy the experience of meditation and devotional songs(Bhajans).

These actions will aid in achieving balance in body, mind, and soul, guiding us towards experiencing ultimate joy.

4) Meditation and Healing: A Positive Direction for Mental Prosperity and Physical Health

Meditation: The Key to Mental Well-being

Meditation is a vital practice for our mental well-being. Through it, we can empower our body, mind, and soul. Meditation helps us recognize our inner self and understand the purpose of our life.To maximize the benefits of meditation, it is crucial to also cultivate mindfulness. We should remember that the objective of meditation is to connect with our soul, not just to achieve concentration.

By practicing meditation correctly, we can enhance our physical and mental health. It allows us to gain clarity on our life's purpose and view life from a new perspective.Meditation comes in various forms, such as focusing on breath, contemplating thoughts, and more. However, it's important to choose a method that feels natural and allows for consistent practice.

Healing: Balancing the Body and Mind

Healing, both physical and mental, is achievable through holistic approaches. Incorporating practices like yoga, mindful breathing, and positive affirmations contribute to the overall well-being.Understanding that our body and mind are interconnected enables us to address health issues comprehensively. A healthy mind positively influences the body, and vice versa. Therefore, embracing a balanced lifestyle that includes meditation and healing practices is essential for a harmonious life.

As we navigate the path of meditation and healing, let's embark on a journey toward holistic well-being, where the mind, body, and soul coexist in a state of equilibrium and vitality.

5) Meditation: An Extraordinary Form of Healing

Understanding Meditation as a Form of Healing

One way to understand meditation is as a means of supporting both spiritual and physical health. While it may not serve as a sole remedy for any illness, studies suggest that regular meditation practice can offer several health-related benefits:

1. **Stress Reduction**: Meditation can assist in reducing stress by enhancing relaxation and helping individuals manage their stress responses effectively.

2. **Anxiety and Depression**: Some studies indicate that regular meditation practice may help alleviate symptoms of anxiety and depression. Meditation encourages individuals to focus on the present moment, fostering a sense of peace and reducing excessive worry.

3. **Enhanced Emotional Well-being**: Meditation practices often involve promoting positive emotions, empathy, and compassion. Regular meditation can lead to improved emotional well-being and a more positive outlook on life.

4. **Improved Sleep**: Meditation can contribute to tranquility and enhance the quality of sleep. It may be beneficial in managing sleep-related issues and other sleep disorders.

5. **Pain Management**: Meditation techniques, such as Mindfulness-Based Stress Reduction (MBSR), are being utilized as part of pain management programs. By increasing awareness and altering perceptions of pain, individuals may experience a reduction in pain intensity.

6. Enhanced Cognitive Abilities: Some studies suggest that the practice of meditation can enhance cognitive functions such as attention, memory, and executive functioning.

Self-Exploration: The Significance of Meditation

In the journey of life, humans explore various aspects, but often, they are not adept at exploring within themselves. Our happiness lies within, and the best way to discover it is through meditation. It provides us with an accessible path to connect with the universe and the divine. Regular meditation nourishes our mental health and intellect in the right measure, allowing us to experience the joy of contentment.

If we encounter any illness, meditation can provide relief, helping us steer clear of falling into the trap of excessive suffering. Continuous meditation grants us the peace that is intrinsic to human life.

6) Meditation: A Therapeutic System for Mental Well-being

Establishing the Habit of Meditation

To cultivate the habit of meditation, we need to follow the mantra "A little but today." In the initial days, we can attempt to meditate for five minutes, but the key is to start today. We must remember, "Do a little, but do it today, not tomorrow."For meditation, it's essential to allocate a specific place and time. Consistency in choosing the same place and time helps ensure that our meditation is effective. It's crucial to start it correctly, especially in the early days.

There are various paths for meditation, such as guided meditation, non-guided meditation, and different meditations by spiritual leaders like Sirshreeji (Happy thoughts available on [YouTube]https://www.tejgyan.org/)). We can derive benefits from these practices.

7) Positive Mentality: Charting the Course to Self-Empowerment

Positive Thinking: Viewing Life from a Positive Perspective

Having a positive mindset or a positive outlook is extremely crucial in human life. In today's stress-filled and worry-laden existence, negativity seems to surround us everywhere. As we wake up, the newspapers and news channels bombard us with negativity, influencing us significantly. Therefore, it's imperative to embrace positivity in every event, with every person, and in every situation.

Negativity can also be transformed into positivity. By accepting events as they are, we can change our mindset to a positive one. If we acknowledge situations as they are, we can transform our thinking positively, leading to positive outcomes.

8) Positive Mentality: Essential for Happiness and Prosperity in Life

As observed, negative events persist in our lives, and some events, due to negative thinking, attract negativity into our lives, adversely affecting our physical and mental health. Therefore, it is crucial to accept every event with ease. If we can accept events correctly, the issue transforms positively, leading to a positive response in our physical and mental well-being.

9) Building Positive Mentality: Study of Self-Motivation and Practical Solutions

Developing Positive Thinking

Viewing life from a positive perspective makes everything better in our lives. Let's contemplate how to develop positive thinking. To achieve this, we need to make our thoughts positive. Being around people with positive thinking and reading books on positive subjects is essential. Using positive affirmations or self-talk consistently in the morning and evening teaches us to adopt a positive perspective in the areas of our physical, mental, social, economic, and spiritual aspects. We need to engage in conversations with positive thoughts and express them in writing. Besides, studying positive literature from leaders worldwide can provide valuable lessons.

FOUR

CHAPTER 4: NATUROPATHY NATURAL HEALING - CONTINUITY WITH ACUPUNCTURE AND SOUND HEALING

1) Natural Healing: Modern Understanding of Natural Elements in Health and Education

Our body is formed from the five basic elements and is a natural marvel. These elements are Earth, Water, Air, Ether, and Fire. Maintaining a balance of these elements in our body is essential, as their imbalance can lead to physical ailments. Following specific practices to keep them balanced is crucial.

In natural healing, these five elements are utilized for therapeutic purposes. Panchakarma, a prominent method in Ayurvedic medicine, involves five major purification processes. This therapeutic approach aims to enhance physical, mental, and spiritual well-being by removing toxic elements from the body.

Panchakarma: Complete Purification of the Body

Panchakarma, an integral part of Ayurvedic medicine, involves five main procedures. The aim of these five activities is to eliminate impurities from the patient's body and restore a balanced state.

1) **Virechana (Purgation Therapy):** In this process, the intake of detoxifying substances helps eliminate waste from the body, ensuring a clean system.

2) **Vamana (Emesis Therapy)**: By ingesting substances from elevated positions, this therapy expels toxins, promoting a cleaner system.

3) **Basti (Enema Therapy)**: Using purified ghee or oil, this therapy regulates the internal and external elimination of waste, based on individual suitability.

4) **Nasya (Nasal Therapy):** Utilizing medicinal substances through the nostrils, this therapy focuses mainly on the upper part of the body.

5) **Raktamokshana (Bloodletting Therapy):** In this process, a controlled amount of blood is withdrawn, ensuring the blood remains clean and healthy.

Adopting these Panchakarma practices can contribute to maintaining good physical and mental health. These methods not only safeguard our well-being but also serve as remedies for various ailments.

2) Natural Healing: Uniqueness of Health and Balance in Modern Lifestyle

First and foremost, it is essential to stay healthy because a lack of health can lead us towards illnesses. The root cause of these illnesses often lies in the absence of genes and natural elements. When we use natural elements correctly, we can stay healthy and keep illnesses at bay.

The balance of the three doshas - Vata, Kapha, and Pitta - in our body, achieved through the balance of the five elements, brings us the joy of health. By utilizing these natural elements correctly, we can free ourselves from the need for medication and enjoy a healthy life. This maintains equilibrium in our body, mind, and soul, allowing us to experience complete well-being.

3) Natural Healing: Ways to Increase Awareness of Health Harmony

Everything in nature is abundant, such as air, water, sunlight, and more. Humans have divided resources, and we need to open our minds to remove these divisions. We should respect every object created by nature. Reading literature on natural healing and experiencing it firsthand by visiting a naturopathy center at least once a year can help us appreciate the benefits.

We should engage in the practices and lifestyle followed in these centers. There is no need to wait until we fall sick; spending a few days at a naturopathy center allows us to understand the natural healing process. By adopting the habits and diet followed there, we can incorporate that lifestyle into our homes. Initiating a regular system for ourselves, our families, and society can contribute to improving overall health.

ShivambuChikitsa: The Ancient Art of Urine Therapy

"ShivambuChikitsa" is an ancient and unique healing method where an individual's own urine (Shivambu) is utilized as the primary treatment. This therapeutic approach finds mention in Ayurveda as an oral tradition and is well-regarded for providing various health benefits, particularly enhancing health through the use of urine-related practices.

The core principle of ShivambuChikitsa is the belief that various health issues and disorders in the body can be treated by consuming urine. It encompasses the method of drinking urine, understanding the right time for it, and evaluating the health benefits derived from it. This therapeutic method promotes self-reliance and encourages individuals to understand and maintain the balance of their bodily functions.

For more details, you can visit [AnandKunj'swebsite](https://anandkunj.com/treatments/)

EFT (Emotional Freedom Techniques): A Path to Mental Well-being

EFT, or Emotional Freedom Techniques, is a mental health technique aimed at reducing your mental stress and worries. This technique works by tapping on meridians or energy pathways in the body, addressing mental pain, fear, or other negative emotions.

The method guides you to tap on specific acupoints while focusing on your issue, saying, "This is my problem, but I completely accept myself." The primary objective is to enhance both physical and mental health, keeping individuals positive.

Acutouch and Sound Healing: A Unique Journey to Health through Sound

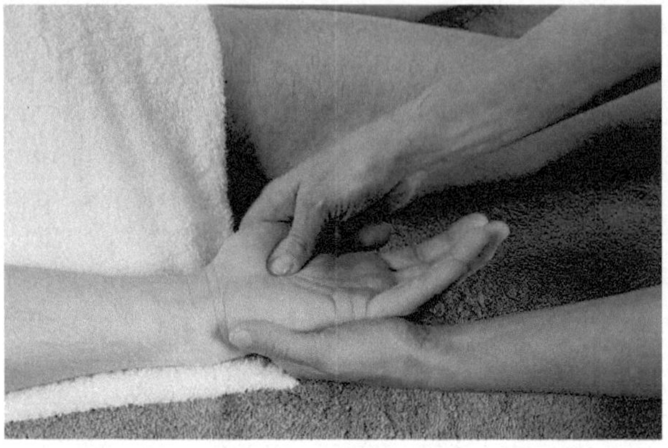

In modern healthcare, Acutouch and Sound Healing represent a novel direction. This distinctive therapy utilizes sound and acoustic techniques to aid in the treatment of various ailments.

Significance of Acutouch:

In Acutouch, musical compositions of various sounds and tones are used for the treatment of illnesses. It incorporates musical therapy, the art of tones, and the use of musical instruments that assist in balancing physical, mental, and spiritual health.

Medium of Sound Healing:

Sound Healing employs the depths of various sounds and tones to heal ailments. This healing method utilizes various instruments, such as Tibetan singing bowls, crystal bowls, and sound baths with tuning forks, to promote overall well-being.

Health Benefits: The Integration of Acutouch and Sound Healing

The combination of Acutouch and Sound Healing can provide physical relief, eliminate energy blockages, and contribute to spiritual well-being. With focused meditation and heightened self-awareness, this therapeutic approach has improved individual and social health.

Sound Healing: A New Perspective on the Journey to Health

Introducing a modern perspective that highlights the specific use of Acutouch and Sound techniques. This guides towards a positive and healthful life, assisting in physical, mental, and spiritual development.

Our body contains crucial points that, when touched or tapped, aid in the proper and seamless functioning of our physical system. Understanding these vital points and applying pressure to them is essential for us. Some points are found in the palm's mudras, while others are located in the soles of our feet. Applying pressure correctly to these points is crucial for us.

In conditions such as insomnia, sleep disorders, stress, depression, etc., practices like meditation and sound healing techniques are used. In this technique, a vessel made of metal or a specific material is played in a particular rhythm or time, creating a sense of peace and contentment. These vibrations help us experience health and vitality.

5) Acutouch and Sound Healing: The Necessity and Health-Related Benefits of these Therapies

Acutouch and Sound Healing: Health Enriched with the Sound of the Soul

In modern medicine, Acutouch and Sound Healing are pioneering unique approaches where the energy of sound is harnessed for healing ailments. These special techniques offer unique benefits for enhancing spiritual and physical health.

Necessity of Acutouch and Sound Healing:

1. **Energy Balance**: Acutouch and Sound Healing use the universal structure of sound to improve energy balance.

2. **Health Security**: The sounds and tones utilized in these methods help calm negative elements, contributing to improved health security.

3. **Mental Health**: Sound Healing positively affects mental health, promoting good sleep, mental clarity, and a healthy atmosphere.

4. **Spiritual State**: Acutouch techniques enhance spiritual strength, inspiration, and happiness, enabling individuals to move towards better health.

Benefits:

These therapeutic methods not only aid in physical healing but also contribute to mental and spiritual well-being. The necessity of Acutouch and Sound Healing taps into the inherent beauty and energy of natural forces, empowering the full potential of health.

6) Acutouch and Sound Healing Skills: Practical Tips and Techniques for Health Improvement

Acutouch and Sound Healing bring a blend of relief for short-term health problems through therapies like vocal and music therapy. These methods not only address physical issues but also contribute to spiritual well-being by balancing the soul. The use of specific tones is like a reset button for the mind, clearing mental blocks and fostering positive thoughts. Sound baths, integral to Acutouch, provide a holistic approach, easing various health concerns and promoting overall well-being.

For those curious about these healing methods, diving into Acupressure through platforms like YouTube is a great start. Learning these techniques empowers individuals to take charge of their well-being. In the journey of life, our bodies are naturally healthy, but with age, diseases may surface. Unfortunately, conventional medicines laden with chemicals might pose risks and impact mental health. Conditions like depression and stress may arise.

To break free from these challenges, understanding crucial body points and correctly applying pressure becomes essential. Sound healing contributes to physical well-being by creating therapeutic waves. Embracing these practices becomes a path to enriching not just physical health but mental and spiritual well-being.

Incorporating the principles of Acutouch and Sound Healing into our lives provides a new perspective on health improvement, addressing the holistic aspects of our well-being.

For more details, visit [www.Acuhealinghub.inor (https://www.rupabannur.com).

7) Consistency: The Key to Stability and Success

Consistency is the Key to Success:

Consistency is taught to us from childhood, yet we often forget to apply it in our lives, leading to encounters with failure. To achieve success in any field, we must maintain consistency repeatedly in that field. However, due to a lack of discipline within us and the fast-paced nature of today's world, we are unable to maintain consistency. As a result, we seek shortcuts and end up facing failure.

To instill any habit, we should be prepared to consistently invest time, even if it's for short durations. Whether it's exercise, studying, or any specific task, maintaining consistency allows us to attain success in that area. Allocating a little time consistently and adhering to it is crucial. By spending more time in a particular area consistently, we can achieve success, benefiting not only our health but every aspect of life.

8) The Significance of Consistency: For Stability and Success in Life

Human beings need consistency to be successful in life. We operate in various realms – physical, mental, social, economic, and spiritual. True success comes when an individual becomes successful in every aspect or facet of life. To achieve success, consistency is crucial in every sphere – be it physical, mental, social, economic, or spiritual.

Consistency in developing good habits is necessary for obtaining success in every dimension of our lives. Whether it's physical health, mental well-being, social harmony, economic prosperity, or spiritual growth, consistent efforts help build positive habits within us. Becoming trustworthy in the eyes of others and enhancing our capabilities, we can progress towards overall development. Consistency is the key to stability and success in all aspects of life.

9. Developing Awareness for Consistency:

Consistency - An Essential Attribute:

Consistency is a crucial attribute that keeps us steadfast in the pursuit of our goals. It aids individuals in maintaining stability despite hard work, struggles, and challenges. Practicing consistency plays a pivotal role in self-discipline and success.

How to Cultivate Awareness for Consistency:

1. Health Awareness:

Regularly engage in exercise and maintain a proper diet. Both physical and mental well-being contribute to consistency.

2. Set Clear Goals:

Define clear and measurable goals and stay committed to achieving them. This will guide you towards consistency.

3. Time Management:

Effectively manage your time and allocate it to tasks of highest priority. This contributes to stability.

4. Self-Dedication:

Demonstrate complete dedication in your endeavors and strive for excellence in every task.

5. Self-Study and Meditation:

Practice self-study and meditation for personal development. This strengthens your consciousness and aids in self-control.

Conclusion:

To develop consistency, it's essential to embrace a healthy lifestyle and commit to regular efforts. This involves adopting a firm resolution and cultivating self-discipline, leading to success. Consistency paves the way for self-dedication and a path towards accomplishment.

FIVE

Chapter 5: Principles of a Healthy Life

1. Healthy and Natural Living: The Path without Medicines

In today's era, there is a lack of discipline within humans. Everyone seeks shortcuts in everything and is ready to do anything for it. Our body can naturally keep itself healthy, but for minor ailments like cold, cough, headache, or any pain, we immediately rush to the pharmacy to get medicines for instant relief. However, we don't realize how many chemical toxins we are introducing into our bodies, and the consequences become apparent only after a long period, with no real benefits. Health is our inherent right, and there's no need for any medication; we can live a completely disease-free life.

2. Medication-Free Life: Ensuring Health by Reducing Medication Use

Maintaining good health is the birthright of every human. However, in today's times, pollution has spread in the air, water, and food, accumulating toxins in our bodies daily. As a result, we are becoming prone to diseases, and for this, we keep taking medicines, which have adverse effects on our bodies. Therefore, living a life free from medication is necessary. Living without medicines ensures that no issues arise in our lives, and we can unlock the full potential of our given bodies.

3. Medication-Free Life: Skill of Supporting Health Without Medicines

To live a healthy life, we need to make some changes. We need constant discipline within us. Waking up early, meditating, going for a morning walk, practicing yoga and pranayama, affirming positive thoughts, reading books, staying in the company of positive people, avoiding prolonged sitting, taking steps instead of using elevators, having meals at the right time, drinking an adequate amount of water, getting good sleep, adopting positive thinking, reading self-reflection books, and watching comedy series and movies—all these changes can help us in the direction of a healthy and positive life.

Nowadays, a new and improved perspective is emerging in the field of personal health and alternative treatments, known as "Medication-Free Life." It is an approach that aligns with modern lifestyles and aims to support health by reducing the use of medicines.

Benefits of Medication-Free Life:

1. **Natural Healing**: Utilizing natural remedies such as Ayurveda and homeopathy provides an effective way to treat illnesses without the use of medicines.

2. **Diet and Exercise**: Following a healthy diet and regular exercise, viewed as excellent alternatives to medication, contributes positively to improving health.

3. **Yoga and Meditation**: Practicing yoga and meditation for mental well-being can be part of holistic treatment without the reliance on medication.

4. **Awareness of Natural Remedies**: Educating people about various natural remedies, including home remedies and Ayurvedic solutions, can contribute to health support.

Living Without Medicines: A Guide to Healthier Living" introduces a fresh approach to boost health without relying on medications. It suggests ways to reduce dependence on drugs and offers tips for natural and spiritual remedies. The goal is to promote a balanced and harmonious life, helping people connect with their inner selves for overall well-being.

NIRVANA

shutterstock.com

4) Health and Spirituality: A Direction towardsa Prosperous and Balanced Life

There exists a profound connection between physical health and spirituality. When our physical health is maintained, our mental well-being also tends to flourish. We come to this earth to learn and discover the purpose of our lives. Consequently, maintaining bodily health becomes a crucial step on the path of spiritual evolution.

Setting a goal for any endeavor and understanding the methods to achieve it is essential. Recognizing and understanding this is true spirituality. Embracing the contributions made to identifying your life's purpose and facing challenges to attain it is the true direction of spiritual progress.

The body is provided to us as a means to reach that goal. Therefore, it is necessary to ensure physical health so that we can leverage our full potential and be capable of achieving our spiritual objectives.

5) Health and Spirituality: The Significance of Spiritual and Physical Balance in Life

Both health and spirituality are essential aspects of our lives. Looking at reality, physical health and spirituality are two sides of the same coin, guiding us toward a balanced way of living. Both body and spirituality are vital facets of our lives. Spirituality involves the exploration of self and understanding one's soul, while the body acts as a medium in this process. Maintaining physical health is crucial for efficiently navigating the moments of our lives and succeeding in our spiritual goals.

By utilizing our bodies correctly, we can attain the highest potential in our lives. Properly managing our physical well-being enables us to make the most of our time in this life, aiding us in being successful in our spiritual objectives. Neglecting our physical health can hinder our success in spiritual pursuits. Therefore, maintaining physical health aligns the path of our spiritual progress with tranquility and balance. Attending to physical health can assist us in achieving our spiritual goals, leading to a balanced and prosperous life.

6) Health and Spirituality: Exploring Balance in the Pursuit of a Happy Life

Health and spirituality are two crucial realms that profoundly influence and shape human life:

1. Health:

Health stands as one of the most significant assets in human life. It encompasses physical, mental, and spiritual well-being, providing support for a joyous and thriving existence. Practices such as maintaining a healthy diet, regular exercise, and engaging in yoga contribute to ensuring health. A healthy lifestyle can also help control issues like depression, stress, and other mental challenges.

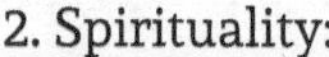

2. Spirituality:

Spirituality redirects human life towards the direction of wonder and elevation. It inspires us toward interpersonal connections, ideals, and self-development. Spiritual experiences can be attained through practices such as meditation, prayer, and religious rituals. Spirituality can assist an individual in understanding the values, purpose, and nature of life, providing support in maintaining peace and balance.

The body is considered a dwelling place for the divine. If we do not litter sacred places like temples, our bodies, which house the divine essence, should be treated with the same reverence. The soul resides within, and it is not appropriate to pollute it. For instance, wrong habits and addictions like tobacco and alcohol can introduce negativity and weakness into our bodies. It is necessary to use our bodies correctly to comprehend our souls.

To maintain physical health properly, practices such as meditation, contemplation, study, reflection, and associating with the wise are necessary. These practices should be a consistent part of our routine, enabling us to view our lives from a spiritual perspective and be successful in attaining our souls. Therefore, maintaining physical health provides guidance toward spiritual progress and aids us in engaging in a dialogue with our souls. By balancing the body and soul, we can experience prosperity and happiness.

7) Health and Treatment: The Final Resort and Last Turn

Humans should consider their body and mind as a powerful instrument, capable of overcoming any challenges. Conscious and subconscious powers reside within the mind, and by utilizing them, remarkable feats can be accomplished. The power of the conscious mind is capable of healing every illness. We need to awaken our consciousness and dedicate ourselves to our physical and mental health.

By using the power of our mind correctly, we can stay healthy, vibrant, and robust. This power can also be harnessed to help ourselves and others. Additionally, scientific research has proven its effectiveness in treating various diseases.

Therefore, we should dedicate our soul to true health and well-being, ensuring that we keep ourselves and others free from ailments.

8) Health and Treatment: Why are the Last Means Important?

Last-resort measures in health are crucial for achieving life goals. By relying on them, we can easily fulfill various aspects of our lives—physical, mental, social, economic, and spiritual. Utilizing our conscious mind effectively helps maintain personal health and contributes to a healthy society.

9) Health and Treatment: How to Develop Optimal Practices?

Developing optimal practices in the field of health and treatment is crucial for people to improve their lifestyles and maintain good health. Here are some important steps that can be taken:

1. Promoting a Healthy Lifestyle:

- Encouraging a balanced diet, regular exercise, and adequate sleep contributes to the promotion of a healthy lifestyle.

2. Self-Dedication:

- Being committed to good health, such as regular check-ups and following health safety guidelines, is vital.

3. Embracing Science and Technological Updates:

- Studying new technological and scientific advancements can lead to advancements in health services.

4. Community Participation:

- Enhancing health participation within community groups can establish a robust health system.

5. Education and Awareness:

- Organizing programs to educate and raise awareness about the importance of health is necessary.

6. Significance of Relationships:

- Maintaining vibrant connections with family, friends, and the community provides support for staying healthy.

In summary, providing information and guidance toward a better and balanced health system, understanding various aspects and ideals that steer individuals towards a healthier life, and proposing ways to enhance improvements in health services, all contribute to the development of optimal health and treatment practices.

Health and Treatment Path: Easy Tips and Regular Habits

1. Wake up Early and Establish a Routine:

- Wake up early and establish a regular daily routine.

2. Incorporate Gratitude:

- Make gratitude a part of your life, for everyone.

3. Support Meditation, Yoga, and Pranayama:

- Support practices like meditation, yoga, and pranayama.

4. Enhance Positive Communication and Reflection:

- Increase positive interactions and practice mindfulness.

5. Make Prayer and Forgiveness Integral:

- Integrate prayer and forgiveness into your life.

6. Adopt a Healthy Lifestyle:

- Embrace a healthy lifestyle and prioritize meditation for peace.

7. Focus on Five Pillars (Food, Water, Sleep, Exercise, Positive Thinking):

- Pay attention to the five main pillars for overall well-being.

Nirvana

Nirvana is a concept in both Buddhist and Hindu philosophies that inspires the soul towards complete liberation and enlightenment. The word originates from Sanskrit, meaning 'freedom from cycles' or 'liberation.' According to the principles of Nirvana, it is a state where the soul is liberated from the bonds of the material world, attaining infinite peace and the perfection of the soul.

To achieve Nirvana, various spiritual paths are followed, such as Karma Yoga, Bhakti Yoga, Jnana Yoga, and meditation. By adhering to these paths, an individual purifies the soul and approaches the state of Nirvana.

Some significant aspects of Nirvana include:

1. **State of Liberation (Moksha):**

- Nirvana is a state where the soul, freed from the cycles of existence, attains profound peace and perfection.

2. **Karma Yoga and Jnana Yoga:**

- Various paths, including Karma Yoga (the path of selfless action) and Jnana Yoga (the path of knowledge), lead to Nirvana.

3. **Perfection of the Soul:**

- In Nirvana, the soul reaches its state of perfection, shedding all afflictions and ignorance.

4. **Attainment of True Knowledge:**

- Nirvana grants the soul true knowledge and awareness, leading to freedom from delusion, ignorance, and suffering.

This spiritual concept holds a significant place in Buddhism, Hinduism, and Jainism, guiding life towards liberation and the realization of the ultimate truth.We have made the term "Nirvana" quite complicated, which needs to be understood correctly. The attainment of liberation, meaning living our human life that we have received in the right way, is necessary. In this, we should achieve victory over our imperfections, maintaining equal empathy towards all beings. This helps us live our lives meaningfully, and with the assistance of a live guru in our life, who can make our life purposeful, we can progress towards the state of Nirvana with heightened consciousness in that journey. With the help of Mahaasmani Shivir offered by Tejgyan Foundation, we can embark on our spiritual journey and transform our lives. Happy thoughts.

for more details of Mahaasmani shivir please visit https://gethappythoughts.org

Conclusion: Health And Spirituality

In this journey, we have taken a step towards understanding health and spirituality, offering a new perspective on life.In today's fast-paced lifestyle, the significance of health and happiness holds a crucial place. The foundation of a joyful life lies in a healthy body, where the right physical capabilities and mental balance play a vital role. Understanding and addressing physical ailments is a significant step towards a healthy life. Including the right nutritional elements in our diet is also a crucial secret to a healthy life.

Maintaining the balance of relationships between the body, mind, and soul is equally essential for the attainment of a harmonious and content life. Recognizing the importance of meditation as a medicine and shaping life positively through constructive thinking are significant steps towards creating a beautiful and positive life.By understanding the principles of natural healing and embracing practices like Ayurveda, one can maintain health in the right way. Living a medication-free life aligns with the pursuit of spiritual and physical well-being. Moreover, the search for Nirvana, for the peace and perfection of the soul, can make life purposeful.

Looking at our lives as a grand picture, where elements like nature, nourishment, care, natural healing, and the pursuit of Nirvana create a beautiful symphony. This narrative is our journey towards prosperity, and our life is influenced by all these elements. Nourishment provides us with energy necessary for our physical and mental health. Understanding the body's natural intelligence through natural healing and the protection of elements from the environment is crucial.

As we move towards Nirvana, all these elements come together for a transformative journey. Nirvana doesn't merely mean a goal; it's a spiritual truth that explains both the physical and spiritual aspects of life. It involves the amalgamation of principles of nature, care, nourishment, and natural healing, guiding us towards a simple and harmonious journey towards prosperity. It connects the body, mind, and soul, harmoniously linking us with the universe.

Wishing you all a fulfilling and healthy life. Thank you. **Stay healthy, stay vibrant, stay robust, and stay happy.**

Sunil Govind Kotwal

www.ingramcontent.com/pod-product-compliance
Lightning Source LLC
LaVergne TN
LVHW041252150826
845673LV00008B/2561
* 9 7 9 8 8 9 3 2 2 3 2 8 6 *